EEYORE
LOSES A TAIL

PLEZ CNOKE
IF AN RNSR
IS NOT REQID

EEYORE
LOSES A TAIL

A.A. MILNE

illustrated by

ERNEST H. SHEPARD

TED SMART

EEYORE
LOSES A TAIL

The Old Grey Donkey, Eeyore, stood by
himself in a thistly corner of the Forest,
his front feet well apart, his head on one
side, and thought about things.
Sometimes he thought sadly to himself,
'Why?' and sometimes he thought,
'Wherefore?' and sometimes he thought,
'Inasmuch as which?' — and sometimes
he didn't quite know what he *was* thinking
about. So when Winnie-the-Pooh came

stumping along, Eeyore was very glad to be able to stop thinking for a little, in order to say 'How do you do?' in a gloomy manner to him.

'And how are you?' said Winnie-the-Pooh.

Eeyore shook his head from side to side.

'Not very how,' he said. 'I don't seem to have felt at all how for a long time.'

'Dear, dear,' said Pooh, 'I'm sorry about that. Let's have a look at you.'

So Eeyore stood there, gazing sadly at the ground, and Winnie-the-Pooh walked all round him once.

'Why, what's happened to your tail?' he said in surprise.

'What *has* happened to it?' said Eeyore.

'It isn't there!'

'Are you sure?'

'Well, either a tail *is* there or it isn't there. You can't make a mistake about it, and yours *isn't* there!'

'Then what is?'

'Nothing.'

'Let's have a look,' said Eeyore, and he turned slowly round to the place where his tail had been a little while ago, and then, finding that he couldn't catch it up, he turned round the other way, until he came back to where he was at first, and then he put his head down and looked between his front legs, and at last he said, with a long, sad sigh, 'I believe you're right.'

'Of course I'm right,' said Pooh.

'That Accounts for a Good Deal,' said

Eeyore gloomily. 'It Explains Everything. No Wonder.'

'You must have left it somewhere,' said Winnie-the-Pooh.

'Somebody must have taken it,' said Eeyore. 'How Like Them,' he added, after a long silence.

Pooh felt that he ought to say something helpful about it, but didn't quite know what. So he decided to do something helpful instead.

'Eeyore,' he said solemnly, 'I, Winnie-the-Pooh, will find your tail for you.'

'Thank you, Pooh,' answered Eeyore. 'You're a real friend,' said he. 'Not Like Some,' he said.

So Winnie-the-Pooh went off to find Eeyore's tail.

It was a fine spring morning in the Forest as he started out. Little soft clouds played happily in a blue sky, skipping from time to time in front of the sun as if they had come to put it out, and then sliding away suddenly so that the next might have his turn. Through them and between them the sun shone bravely; and a copse which had worn its firs all the year round seemed old and dowdy now beside the new green lace which the beeches had put on so prettily. Through copse and spinney marched Bear; down open slopes of gorse and heather, over rocky beds of streams, up steep banks of sandstone into the heather again; and so at last, tired and hungry, to the Hundred Acre Wood. For it was in the Hundred Acre Wood that Owl lived.

'And if anyone knows anything about anything,' said Bear to himself, 'it's Owl who knows something about something,' he said, 'or my name's not Winnie-the-Pooh,' he said. 'Which it is,' he added. 'So there you are.'

Owl lived at The Chestnuts, an old-world residence of great charm, which was grander than anybody else's, or seemed so to Bear, because it had both a knocker *and* a bell-pull. Underneath the knocker there was a notice which said:

PLES RING IF AN RNSER IS REQIRD.

Underneath the bell-pull there was a notice which said:

PLEZ CNOKE IF AN RNSR IS NOT
REQID.

These notices had been written by Christopher Robin, who was the only one in the Forest who could spell; for Owl, wise though he was in many ways, able to read and write and spell his own name WOL, yet somehow went all to pieces over delicate words like MEASLES and BUTTEREDTOAST.

Winnie-the-Pooh read the two notices very carefully, first from left to right, and afterwards, in case he had missed some of it, from right to left. Then, to make quite sure, he knocked and pulled the knocker, and he pulled and knocked the bell-rope, and he called out in a very loud voice, 'Owl! I require an answer! It's Bear speaking.' And the door opened, and Owl looked out.

'Hallo, Pooh,' he said. 'How's things?'

'Terrible and Sad,' said Pooh, 'because Eeyore, who is a friend of mine, has lost his tail. And he's Moping about it. So could you very kindly tell me how to find it for him?'

'Well,' said Owl, 'the customary procedure in such cases is as follows.'

'What does Crustimoney Proseedcake mean?' said Pooh. 'For I am a Bear of Very Little Brain, and long words Bother me.'

'It means the Thing to Do.'

'As long as it means that, I don't mind,' said Pooh humbly.

'The thing to do is as follows. First, Issue a Reward. Then —'

'Just a moment,' said Pooh, holding up his paw. '*What* do we do to this — what you were saying? You sneezed just as you were going to tell me.'

'I *didn't* sneeze.'

'Yes, you did, Owl.'

'Excuse me, Pooh, I didn't. You can't sneeze without knowing it.'

'Well, you can't know it without something having been sneezed.'

'What I *said* was, "First *Issue* a Reward".'

'You're doing it again,' said Pooh sadly.

'A Reward!' said Owl very loudly. 'We
write a notice to say that we will give a
large something to anybody who finds
Eeyore's tail.'

'I see, I see,' said Pooh, nodding his
head. 'Talking about large somethings,'
he went on dreamily, 'I generally have a
small something about now — about this
time in the morning,' and he looked

wistfully at the cupboard in the corner of Owl's parlour; 'just a mouthful of condensed milk or what-not, with perhaps a lick of honey —'

'Well, then,' said Owl, 'we write out this notice, and we put it up all over the Forest.'

'A lick of honey,' murmured Bear to himself, 'or — or not, as the case may be.' And he gave a deep sigh, and tried very hard to listen to what Owl was saying.

But Owl went on and on, using longer and longer words, until at last he came back to where he started, and he explained that the person to write out this notice was Christopher Robin.

'It was he who wrote the ones on my front door for me. Did you see them, Pooh?'

For some time now Pooh had been saying 'Yes' and 'No' in turn, with his eyes shut, to all that Owl was saying, and having said, 'Yes, yes,' last time, he said, 'No, not at all,' now, without really knowing what Owl was talking about.

'Didn't you see them?' said Owl, a little surprised. 'Come and look at them now.'

So they went outside. And Pooh looked at the knocker and the notice below it, and he looked at the bell-rope and the notice below it, and the more he looked at

PLEZ CNOKE
IF AN RNSR
IS NOT REQID

the bell-rope, the more he felt that he had seen something like it, somewhere else, sometime before.

'Handsome bell-rope, isn't it?' said Owl.

Pooh nodded.

'It reminds me of something,' he said, 'but I can't think what. Where did you get it?'

'I just came across it in the Forest. It was hanging over a bush, and I thought at first somebody lived there, so I rang it, and nothing happened, and then I rang it again very loudly, and it came off in my hand, and as nobody seemed to want it, I took it home, and —'

'Owl,' said Pooh solemnly, 'you made a mistake. Somebody did want it.'

'Who?'

'Eeyore. My dear friend Eeyore. He was — he was fond of it.'

'Fond of it?'

'Attached to it,' said Winnie-the-Pooh
sadly.

So with these words he unhooked it, and
carried it back to Eeyore; and when
Christopher Robin had nailed it on in its
right place again, Eeyore frisked about
the Forest, waving his tail so happily that

Winnie-the-Pooh came over all funny,
and had to hurry home for a little snack
of something to sustain him. And, wiping
his mouth half an hour afterwards, he
sang to himself proudly:

Who found the Tail?
   'I,' said Pooh,
'At a quarter to two
   (Only it was quarter to eleven really),
   I found the Tail!'

LINES WRITTEN BY
A BEAR OF VERY LITTLE BRAIN

On Monday, when the sun is hot
I wonder to myself a lot:
'Now is it true, or is it not,
'That what is which and which is what?'

On Tuesday, when it hails and snows,
The feeling on me grows and grows
That hardly anybody knows
If those are these or these are those.

On Wednesday, when the sky is blue,
And I have nothing else to do,
I sometimes wonder if it's true
That who is what and what is who.

On Thursday, when it starts to freeze
And hoar-frost twinkles on the trees,
How very readily one sees
That these are whose — but whose are these?

On Friday —

HOW SWEET TO BE
A CLOUD

How sweet to be a Cloud
  Floating in the Blue!
Every little cloud
Always sings aloud.

'How sweet to be a Cloud
  Floating in the Blue!'
It makes him very proud
To be a little cloud.

ISN'T IT FUNNY?

Isn't it funny
How a bear likes honey?
Buzz! Buzz! Buzz!
I wonder why he does?

COTTLESTON PIE

Cottleston, Cottleston, Cottleston Pie.
A fly can't bird, but a bird can fly.
Ask me a riddle and I reply:
'*Cottleston, Cottleston, Cottleston Pie.*'

Cottleston, Cottleston, Cottleston Pie,
A fish can't whistle and neither can I.
Ask me a riddle and I reply:
'*Cottleston, Cottleston, Cottleston Pie.*'

Cottleston, Cottleston, Cottleston Pie,
Why does a chicken, I don't know why.
Ask me a riddle and I reply:
'*Cottleston, Cottleston, Cottleston Pie.*'

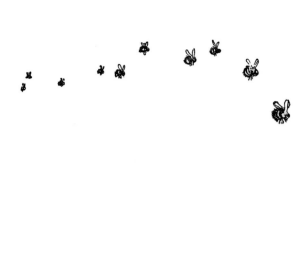

Eeyore Loses a Tail
is taken from *Winnie-the-Pooh*
originally published in Great Britain 14th October 1926
by Methuen & Co. Ltd.
Text by A.A.Milne and line drawings by Ernest H.Shepard
copyright under the Berne Convention

First published 1991 by Methuen Children's Books
an imprint of Egmont Children's Books Limited
239 Kensington High Street, London W8 6SA

This edition first produced in 1998 for The Book People
Hall Wood Avenue, Haydock, St Helens WA11 9UL

ISBN 1 85613 414 8

3 5 7 9 10 8 6 4

Printed in Hong Kong